This book belongs to:

....

....

....

Stories for 7 Year Olds

Written by Nicola Baxter,
Moira Butterfield, Marcel Feigel,
Jan and Tony Payne

Illustrated by Jane Cope
(Linda Rogers Associates)

Designed by Blue Sunflower Creative

This is a Parragon book
This edition published in 2006

Parragon
Queen Street House
4 Queen Street
Bath BA1 1HE, UK

ISBN 1-40544-723-0
Printed in England

Stories for 7 Year Olds

p

Contents

Never Kiss a Frog!

"There's no way that I would ever kiss a frog," said Sarah.

"Nor me," said Emma.

"That's revolting," shuddered Allie.

"Completely gross," agreed Sarah.

"I'd rather kiss Knobbly Norman," said Emma, pulling a face.

"Yuck!" giggled the three girls together.

"What about you, Rachel?" Allie asked. "Would you kiss a frog?"

"I wouldn't mind!" said Rachel calmly. "I like frogs."

The three girls stared at her. Rachel stared calmly back. "It wouldn't be a big deal," she said. "I'd do it if I had to."

The girls had been reading ***The Frog***

Prince. Of course, it was just a fairy story, but they were on the side of the princess. Kissing frogs was something they would never, ever do. Never in a million years.

Except Rachel.

"OK," said Sarah, "Let's see you do it."

"Yes, let's see you," said Allie, "And not a baby frog either. It's got to be a big, fat, slimy frog."

"Yes, a slimy, green frog, with dribble coming out of its mouth." The girls pulled disgusted faces and shrieked with laughter.

"OK," said Rachel. "You choose the frog, and I'll kiss it. You never know, it may turn into a prince!"

The next day the girls had a nature class at school. Miss Gaston took them for a walk in the fields near the river.

"Children!" she called, stopping and bending over to look at something on the ground. "Do any of you know what this is?"

The children stood around her and stared at a brown insect half hiding under some leaves.

"I think it's a stag beetle, Miss," said a bony-faced boy. It was Knobbly Norman.

Emma gave a loud snort, which she quickly turned into a cough. Miss Gaston frowned at her.

"Well done, Norman," she said. "It is indeed a stag beetle. Now, all of you, listen carefully..." and she went on to tell them all about the habits of the stag beetle. The four girls soon lost interest. They had something else on their minds.

"Miss Gaston," said Allie, "are there any frogs around here?"

"There should be," said Miss Gaston. "Frogs like to live near water."

It wasn't until they were sitting eating their sandwiches that they heard a croaking sound followed by loud plops.

They watched as a whole family of frogs hopped down the river bank and jumped into the water. None of them was very big or very revolting.

"One of those will do," said Rachel, pointing to a small frog.

"Oh no it won't," chorused the others. And they started to hunt among the reeds at the river's edge.

They soon found the perfect frog. He was large and fat. When one of the girls touched him his skin felt damp and clammy. He didn't seem to want to get into the water with the other frogs. He just sat on the grass, staring at them.

Sarah picked him up between two paper tissues and sat him in her empty lunchbox. The frog kept perfectly still. He seemed completely at home. The girls looked from him to Rachel.

"He's a beauty," said Allie.

"He's perfect," agreed Emma.

"Ready, Rachel?" asked Sarah.

Rachel took the lunchbox on her lap. Tossing back her hair, she closed her eyes, screwed up her face and leant forward. The frog waited expectantly. He had a gleam in his eye. And as Rachel bent over to kiss him, he raised his head, puckered his lips and...KISSED HER BACK!

With a cry Rachel jumped up and the lunchbox slid off her lap onto the ground.

"Ugh!" she said. "Ugh!" And she scrubbed furiously at her lips with a tissue.

"You did it," cried Emma, clapping her hands. "You did it!"

"Brilliant," said Allie.

"Ugh!" repeated Rachel, still scrubbing her face. "That was disgusting. The horrible thing tried to kiss me back."

"Rubbish," said Emma.

"You imagined it," said Allie.

"Perhaps he's going to turn into a prince," joked Sarah.

They looked at the frog. He was still sitting there staring at nothing with his unblinking eyes. The girls gathered up their things and ran off. The frog watched as they joined the rest of the class. Then he jumped out of the lunchbox and, with little flippety, floppety sounds, he started to hop after them.

The next morning Rachel woke in a good mood. She was looking forward to school today. There was an art lesson in the afternoon, and she had some really cool new trainers. She was singing as she got dressed. But when she went into the bathroom to clean her teeth, she had the shock of her life. Sitting on her face cloth was the frog! The same frog she had kissed yesterday. She stared at him with a horrified expression. The frog stared back with that same unblinking stare. Then, horror of horrors, he lifted his head and puckered his lips! He wanted another kiss!!

With a cry Rachel dropped the toothbrush and dashed downstairs. In the kitchen Mum and Dad were eating breakfast.

"What's wrong?" asked Mum.

"There's a frog in the bathroom," gasped Rachel.

"***Honestly*** Rachel," said Dad.

"There *is* – get rid of it!" cried Rachel.

"I'll go," said Mum. Minutes later she came back with the frog in her hand. "He's quite harmless," she said to Rachel.

The frog sat perfectly still in the palm of Mum's hand. He looked at Rachel with a smug smile.

"Put him in the garden," pleaded Rachel. "Please."

"OK," said Mum, going out. "But he's not going to hurt you, you know."

"I didn't know you were scared of frogs," said Dad.

"I wasn't, I mean, I'm not," said Rachel, and leaving it at that she sat down to eat some breakfast.

Once at school everything was fine. Rachel and her friends always had a good time together. Today Emma made her laugh when she scribbled a drawing on her notepad of Miss Gaston kissing the frog. Underneath she had written 'Gasbags and her boyfriend'.

But apart from that, no one mentioned what had happened the day before. And Rachel didn't say anything about seeing the frog again that morning. She was beginning to think she had imagined the whole thing. It couldn't have been the same frog. Freaky things like that just don't happen.

In the afternoon the class got ready for their art lesson. They were going to draw a real person. Rachel had volunteered to sit for them. Miss Gaston asked her to sit behind a desk in front of the class and rest her chin on her hand.

The class got out pads and pencils and Rachel got into position. It was difficult to keep still and at first she fidgeted quite a lot. Once, when Miss Gaston wasn't looking, she took her chin off her hand, put a finger in each corner of her mouth and pulled a face. The class sniggered.

"Settle down, children," said Miss Gaston, unaware of Rachel's antics. "I don't see anything to laugh at. Rachel is a perfectly normal-looking girl."

At this there was a loud snort from Emma, who quickly got out a handkerchief and tried to turn it into a sneeze.

For a while Rachel behaved herself and the class got on with their drawing. But sitting still in a warm room, with sunlight filtering in through the windows, made her feel sleepy. She closed her eyes, feeling more and more drowsy. The room was very quiet. All she could hear was the scritch scratch of pencils on paper as the rest of the class drew her. Then she heard a different sound. It seemed to be coming from a long way off. It sounded a bit like the croak of a frog. "Rubbish," she thought to herself, "I've got frogs on the brain." Then she heard it again. It definitely was a croak. She opened her eyes, and suddenly she was wide awake. Sitting on the table in front of her, its eyes fixed on her face, was the frog she had seen in the bathroom that morning. The very same one she had kissed the day before.

A voice piped up from the class.

"Look, Miss, there's a frog on the table. Shall we draw him as well?" It was Knobbly Norman.

There was pandemonium. Rachel jumped up and overturned the table. Miss Gaston dashed about trying to find the frog, but it had disappeared. Rachel's friends crowded around her.

"Is it the frog from yesterday?" asked Allie. Rachel nodded. "He's following me around," she said.

"He can't be," said Sarah. "Frogs are

stupid. They don't have brains."

"Did you bring that frog into the classroom, Rachel?" asked Miss Gaston sternly, getting up off her hands and knees.

"No, Miss Gaston," replied Rachel.

"Then who did?" asked Miss Gaston, looking at the rest of the class.

"It must have hopped in from outside," said Emma quickly.

Over the next few days Rachel saw the frog loads more times. Once he followed her home from school, hopping a few metres behind her. Once she found him sitting on top of her computer. And, worst of all, one evening when she was getting ready for bed, she found him asleep on her pillow.

She couldn't believe this was happening to her. She was beginning to feel really spooked. She decided to phone her friends and arrange an emergency meeting.

"Come home with me after school tomorrow," she begged them. "I've got something to tell you."

"This is freaky," said Emma, after Rachel had finished telling her what had happened.

"It's just like the story," said Sarah. "You know, ***The Frog Prince***."

"Just as well you didn't promise to marry him," joked Allie.

"What do you think I should do?" asked Rachel.

They were all sitting around the kitchen table. Rachel's mother had left them home-made pizza and a salad.

"We've got to get rid of him," said Emma.

"Ugh! You don't mean...the chop...?" squeaked Allie.

"No, I don't mean...the dreaded chop," said Emma. "Let's take him somewhere, a long way away, and leave him behind."

"Great," said Rachel, clapping her hands.

"Where?" Allie asked.

"I know," said Rachel. "I'm going riding tomorrow. The riding school is miles away. I'll take the frog and leave him there."

"Right," said Sarah. "And I bet that will be the last you see of him."

The next day Mum took Rachel for her riding lesson and on the way home she left the frog at the edge of a nearby stream. He didn't try to follow her. He just watched in silence as she walked back to the car.

Feeling guilty, Rachel turned to look at him before they drove away. It seemed to her that he looked more miserable than she had ever seen him before.

Rachel soon forgot about the frog. Weeks went by and she didn't see him again. Things were back to normal. She saw her friends, she went riding, she watched TV, she went to school. She was her old happy-go-lucky self.

Then one day she went into the garden and saw him sitting by the pond. Her heart sank. The frog looked thinner than the last time she had seen him, but he still looked at her with that same steady, unblinking stare.

"It can't be the same one, can it?" Mum said to Rachel, when she saw him.

"No, it's not the same one," said Rachel. But in her heart she knew it was, and for some unknown reason she felt a

strange feeling of sadness.

The frog stayed by the pond. He was very thin. His mournful eyes followed her about but, instead of hating him like she had done before, Rachel started feeling sorry for him. He looked as though he was fading away.

Then she had an idea.

"He's desperate for a girlfriend," she told her friends. "So let's find him one."

"But he thinks he's got a girlfriend already," said Sarah, pointing at Rachel. Rachel didn't say anything.

"We've got to find him someone he likes even more than Rachel," said Allie.

"What about Gasbags?" joked Emma.

"Be serious," laughed Rachel. "What he needs is another frog."

"Something pretty and cute."

"And irresistible."

"And different."

So the girls set about finding the perfect girlfriend for Rachel's frog. First they tried introducing him to some exotic frogs and toads from the local nature reserve. But none of them seemed to interest him.

The Flying Frog showed him how she could glide from one tree to another but he was unimpressed. He turned his back on the brilliant, Oriental Fire-bellied Toad. He completely ignored the yellow and black Corroboree Frog, even though she had come all the way from Australia. It was the same story with the Ghost Frog and the Leopard Frog and the Glass Frog. The girls thought they were all really cool, but Rachel's frog just couldn't be bothered with any of them.

The girls couldn't think what else to try. The frog just sat by Rachel's pond. He didn't eat and he didn't drink. It seemed as though he was pining away. It made Rachel unhappy to watch him.

Then, one afternoon, the four girls were walking in the park when they heard the sound of singing. It was so faint that at first they thought it was a radio playing a long way off. Then Rachel stopped.

"What's up?" asked Emma.

"Listen!" whispered Rachel.

Some frogs are brown, dilly-dilly,
Some frogs are green,
If you'll be my king, dilly-dilly,
I'll be your queen.

"Did you hear that?" asked Sarah.

The girls nodded.

"It's coming from the pond," said Allie.

Very carefully the girls parted the reeds. There, sitting on a lily pad, they saw a small green frog.

"I think it's just a common frog," said Rachel, who knew quite a bit about frogs by now. "But she's cute, isn't she?"

"Yes, she is," said Emma.

"Do you think it was her singing?" asked Sarah.

"How could it be?" asked Allie. "Frogs don't sing."

"Let's take her back with us, anyway," said Emma. "You never know, Rachel's frog might take a fancy to her."

"I wish you wouldn't call him my frog," said Rachel.

They looked down at the little green frog. She was watching them intently, almost as if she was listening.

"Come on, little frog," said Rachel, picking her up. "Come and meet your handsome prince."

When they got back, Rachel's frog was waiting for them. The girls put the little female frog near to the pond and left them together.

The next day they were nowhere to be seen.

"I still can't believe I've seen the last of him," said Rachel, when she told her friends. But she hoped it was true.

Then, one day, she was out riding her pony. It was a gloomy, misty sort of day and she could hardly see the other riders who were a little ahead of her. She was just about to try and catch up when she heard someone singing. At first she thought it was a song she had heard before, but when she listened carefully she realized she had heard the tune before. Yet the words were different.

I love you so, dilly-dilly,
And I know you love me.
If you'll be mine, dilly-dilly,
How happy we'll be.

The sound was coming from the other side of some bushes. Rachel slipped off her pony and moved quietly forward. It was still very misty but she could just see the shapes of a young man and a woman sitting close together. Both were dressed in fine clothes of silk and satin and on each of their heads was a golden crown. They were so absorbed in each other that they didn't notice her.

Rachel stopped dead. She could hardly believe what she was seeing. Then her pony started to move away and she turned to hold onto his bridle. When she looked back the mist had cleared and the young man and woman had vanished.

On Saturday, Rachel and her friends had a picnic in the garden. Dad had put up a tent and filled the paddling pool. They played outside until it was dark then watched a Harry Potter film on TV.

Rachel's friends congratulated each other on getting rid of the frog at last. They joked that he and the little female frog must be living together in happy froggy land.

Rachel joked with them. She didn't mention what she had seen.

"There's no point in telling them," she thought. "They'll only think I'm mad. And I probably imagined it anyway."

But from that day to this she has never touched, or held, or spoken to another frog.

And she has certainly never kissed one!

Emily Meets a Dancing Spider

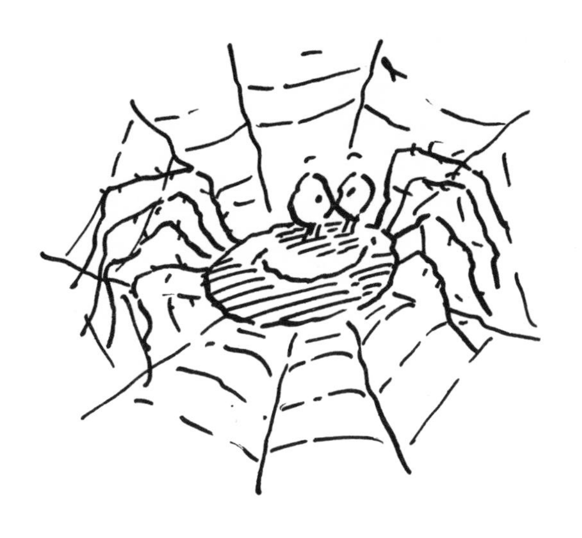

"I'm going to play in the garden," Emily told her mother. It was the start of the school holidays and Emily couldn't wait to play in her tree house. Dad had made it for her birthday and it was the best present she had ever had. She'd really wanted a dog for her birthday but, as usual, her parents had made up an excuse why she couldn't have one.

The tree house was halfway up the oak tree, and you had to climb a little rope ladder to reach it. Inside, there was a table and chairs, and some big soft cushions on the floor. Emily loved it. Sometimes she took her friends up there, and they had yummy picnics that Mum packed for them.

Sometimes her little brother, Raymond, was allowed in the tree house, but he couldn't climb the ladder on his own.

Today, Emily was going to do a flower painting. She climbed up the ladder into the tree house and laid out her paints on the table near the window. Emily loved looking down on the garden from this height. She could see everything so clearly – especially the grass and the flowers below her. The roses were in bloom and so were the sweet peas. Emily loved sweet peas. The colours were so pretty. She decided to draw them. As she sketched, she hummed to herself. Emily was good at making up songs of her own.

As she looked she could see bees and butterflies darting in and out of the sweet peas. Then she saw a butterfly with silvery wings resting right in the centre of a flower. She watched as it fluttered its wings and warmed itself in the sunlight. It was still for a moment, then it lifted its wings again, and this time Emily saw a pink dress that glittered and sparkled in the light. Then she saw a cloud of fine, golden hair. She stared in amazement.

It wasn't a butterfly at all!

It was a fairy!!

"It can't be," gasped Emily to herself. "I must be dreaming."

She closed her eyes, and opened them again, quickly. The fairy was still there. Then Emily saw her open the petals of a flower, and put something inside.

When the fairy had gone Emily climbed down the ladder and went over to the sweet peas. She still half thought she must be dreaming. But when she looked inside the flower she found a tiny piece of paper covered with black spidery writing. It was a letter addressed to her. It said...

Dear Emily,

My name is Fairy Sweet Pea. I live in your garden. I have heard you singing in your tree house. Will you be my friend and write to me?

Love from Sweet Pea

PS Please keep this a secret.

Emily wrote back straight away:

Dear Sweet Pea,

Thank you for your note. I would love to be your friend. Of course I will keep it a secret, especially from my brother Raymond. Raymond is so boring. He collects rubber bands!

Love from Emily

PS Tell me what you do in the garden.

The next day there was another note from Sweet Pea:

Dear Emily,

There is a lot to do in the garden. My job is to paint all the sweet peas a different colour. That is why I'm called Sweet Pea. Then I spray them all with perfume. What do you do in your tree house?

Love Sweet Pea

PS Enclosed is a rubber band for Raymond. Don't tell him it's from me.

Emily answered:

Dear Sweet Pea,

Thank you for the rubber band. I'll tell Raymond I found it. I smelt the sweet peas today. The perfume you put on them is gorgeous. I wish you could come with me to the tree house. You could share my picnic.

Yesterday I had a knickerbocker glory.

Love Emily

PS I paint flowers too. I paint pictures of them in my painting book. I did one of a pink sweet pea. Would you like to see it?

Sweet Pea replied:

Dear Emily,

I would love to see your painting of a pink sweet pea. Pink is my favourite colour. Do you know Sammy Seagull? Yesterday I sprayed him with fairy dust to make him pink. He looked so funny!

Love Sweet Pea

Emily wrote:

Dear Sweet Pea,

Here is the painting I did of a pink sweet pea. I've also done a painting of

Sammy Seagull with pink feathers. I think pink suits him.

Love Emily

Emily and Sweet Pea wrote to each other every day. Emily told Sweet Pea all the things she was doing and Sweet Pea told Emily all the things that she was doing. Then one day, when Emily looked inside the flower, it was empty.

She looked again the next day and the next, but there was nothing there. She looked every day for a week. Had Sweet Pea gone away? Was she ill? Had something happened to her? Emily was worried. She didn't know what to think.

Then one day, there was another note. Excitedly Emily opened it. It didn't say much:

My dear friend Emily,

I need your help. Please meet me,

tonight, behind the white rose bush at the bottom of the garden.

Love from Sweet Pea

PS Don't tell anyone.

That evening, after tea, Emily went into the garden. Nobody saw her go. Mum and Dad were in the kitchen and Raymond was watching television and flicking rubber bands at the screen.

Treading as softly as she could, Emily followed the path that led up to the rose bush. If Sweet Pea was there, she really didn't want to startle her.

Emily heard Sweet Pea before she saw her. The fairy was crying softly to herself. She was sitting under a white rose and she was the loveliest thing Emily had ever seen. Her tiny face was beautiful, and her golden hair reached well below her waist. Her wings were folded behind her back.

The fairy smiled when she saw Emily. Emily held out her hand and Sweet Pea climbed onto it and sat very still. Now that she was so close, Emily could see that the fairy was upset.

"What is the matter, Sweet Pea?" she asked, softly. Sweet Pea said nothing. Instead she slowly opened her wings.

Emily gasped.

Sweet Pea's fine, gossamer wings had been torn to shreds!

"How did it happen?" asked Emily.

"I caught them in some brambles," said Sweet Pea, sadly. Sweet Pea told Emily that she needed some gossamer to repair them.

"What's gossamer?" asked Emily.

"It's the thread that spiders make to spin their webs," explained Sweet Pea.

"Well, there are lots of spiders' webs in the tree house," said Emily. But it wasn't as simple as that. The gossamer had to come from the web of a rare dancing spider. The dancing spider lived in a cave a long way away.

"I've heard that the only way the spider will give up his web is when he is dancing," sighed Sweet Pea. "And the only time he will dance is when someone sings to him."

"So what's the problem?" asked Emily.

"I just can't sing," said Sweet Pea. "Will you come with me?"

"I mustn't be gone long," said Emily.

"If we travel tonight we will be back by the morning," Sweet Pea promised. "Sammy Seagull is going to take us."

That night, Sweet Pea sprinkled Emily

with fairy dust to make her small. Then the two of them climbed onto Sammy's back. He fluffed out his pink feathers to protect his passengers from the cold night air. Then he flapped his wings and headed towards the setting sun.

Sammy flew fast. Emily could see fields and villages far below and pinpricks of light from farms and houses. As they snuggled down in Sammy's warm feathers the first star appeared next to a thin strip of moon. Emily closed her eyes, and soon she had fallen fast asleep.

She woke suddenly to feel Sammy dropping like a stone. "Hold on tight," he shouted.

The ground rose to meet them. It was covered in snow and dotted with mountain peaks that glittered in the moonlight. Sticking both feet straight down in front of him, Sammy landed on the lowest branch of a large tree. The snow on the ground was frozen, and it was very cold. Taking a handful of fairy dust, Sweet Pea magicked thick jumpers for herself and Emily.

The rare spider lived in a cave on the side of the mountain, hidden behind a waterfall. Sweet Pea could hear the sound of water and knew which direction to take. But it was difficult walking in the icy snow.

Sweet Pea found some twigs and a wood beetle. She took another handful of fairy dust and sprinkled it over them. A sleigh and a large dog appeared in their place. The dog was brown with a white patch over one eye. He sat in the snow and looked at them with bright eyes. Emily

loved him at once.

"What's his name?" she asked, putting on her new jumper.

"Bernard," said Sweet Pea.

They harnessed Bernard to the sleigh and set off, a lantern lighting their way. Sweet Pea was pleased with her work. There was only one problem. She had used up almost a whole bag of fairy dust. "I mustn't use any more," she thought. "I might need the rest when we reach the spider." She was afraid that the spider might catch them in his web!

As they approached the cave, the sound of the waterfall was much louder. Bernard was pulling the sleigh along a narrow path between tall trees and all they could see was the dark branches against the night sky. Then they came out into a clearing and the waterfall was in front of them. The sight and the sound made them gasp. The water fell in a torrent down the face of the mountain. It made such a roar that they had to shout to make themselves heard.

"How do we get into the cave?" shouted Emily.

"Behind the waterfall," shouted back Sweet Pea.

They all stared at the wall of water in front of them. Going through it looked impossible. Sweet Pea reached into the bag of fairy dust. She threw the last handful into the waterfall. The water froze instantly, leaving a gap just wide enough for them to walk through into the cave behind.

"The waterfall will stay like this until daylight," said Sweet Pea. "We must be out by then, or we will be trapped with the spider forever."

"Let's go," said Emily, and the four

friends squeezed carefully through the gap in the frozen waterfall.

It was very dark in the cave. Occasionally a bat swooped low and almost touched them. Emily tried not to be scared. She ducked her head and kept as still as possible. Their lantern light flickered on the slimy walls, lighting up all the nooks and crannies.

Then Emily noticed what looked like a huge hammock stretching from one side of the cave to the other. It must be the spider's web.

But it was empty.

"He's not there," whispered Emily.

"Ssshh!" whispered Sweet Pea, listening. There was a rustling noise, and the web began to sway. At first it moved very slowly, as if a giant hand was rocking it backwards and forwards.

Bernard whimpered, covering his eyes

with his paws. Bernard didn't like spiders. Sammy didn't say anything. He had buried his head under his wing.

In silence, Sweet Pea and Emily watched as an enormous spider started pulling himself up the web with his hairy feet. When he reached the middle he sat there, squat and black, staring down at them with cold, dark eyes.

Emily shuddered.

"Do something, Sweet Pea," she whispered. "Make him small with fairy dust."

"I haven't any left," answered Sweet

Pea, feeling scared.

Emily thought quickly. At home, if she was scared of anything, Mum would sing to her, and the scared feeling would go away. Perhaps it would work now.

She started to sing.

At first her voice was wobbly, but the more she sang the stronger it became. Soon the whole cave was filled with the sound of her sweet voice.

The others started to feel better too. Sammy took his head out from under his wing, and Bernard uncovered his eyes. Then something very strange happened. The spider held up his hairy legs, took one or two little steps, and began to dance!

"One, two, three...one, two, three..." he hummed to himself. "One, two, three... one, two, three..."

At first he danced slowly, and then he got faster and faster, spinning round and round the cave until the four friends were dizzy watching him.

Then Sweet Pea noticed that while he was dancing he was also spinning a new web – clouds and clouds of the finest gossamer.

"Keep singing, Emily," she whispered. "We must keep him dancing."

Emily tried to remember all the songs that Mum had taught her and, while she sang, Sweet Pea collected enough gossamer to repair her wings. Then she made a pair for Emily and a pair for Bernard, so they could fly home together. Sammy didn't need any; he already had his own wings.

By now it was almost daylight. Emily had been singing so long her voice was getting croaky. Hardly daring to move she put on her new wings, while Sweet Pea helped Bernard put on his. Then, still singing softly, they started back towards the waterfall. The spider didn't take any notice. He was too busy dancing. But, as the singing got fainter and fainter, he began to slow down and look around him. They had almost reached the gap in the waterfall when the spider made a lightning-fast movement and darted after them. But it was too late. They squeezed through just as the first light began to show in the sky. Once again the water started to cascade down the face of the mountain. The spider was trapped.

Then Emily heard a voice calling.

"Emily! Emily!" called the voice.

Emily blinked. It sounded like Mum. She blinked again.

"Emily! Wake up!" Mum called. "It's time to get dressed." Emily opened her eyes.

She was at home in bed!

Mum came into the room and kissed her. "Up you get, sleepy head," she said. "Your breakfast is ready."

Wide awake, Emily jumped out of bed.

"Why, you're dressed already!" Mum said, in a surprised voice.

Emily looked at herself in the mirror. She was wearing a thick jumper.

"I don't remember that jumper," said Mum in a puzzled voice. "Was it a birthday present from Grandma?"

Emily didn't answer. Carefully she took it off and, as she did, something small and silvery fell to the carpet. It was a tiny pair of gossamer wings! She folded the tiny wings and put them carefully in her jewellery box with all her other treasures.

When she went downstairs, there was another surprise waiting for her. Sitting by the open kitchen door was a large brown dog with a white patch over one eye!

When he saw Emily the dog trotted over and started licking her.

"He seems to know you," said Mum.

Emily gave Bernard a hug. He sat in front of her with his head cocked on one side. Mum smiled at Emily.

"I think he'd better stay," she said, "until we find out where he belongs."

Emily put her arms around Mum and kissed her. "This is where he really belongs," she said. "At home, with us."

Bernard wagged his tail. He couldn't have agreed more.

The Ghost Train

As Lauren and James Brown entered the gates leading to 'Weird World', they knew they were in for a good time.

The place was full of people – weird people!

A man with two heads was selling candyfloss.

Frankenstein's monster was limbo dancing.

Dracula and Mrs Dracula were cooking hamburgers in a little white van. A line of children queued to buy one. As Lauren watched, Mrs Dracula spread blood-red tomato ketchup on a double-whammy burger and then bit into it. The ketchup clung gruesomely to her long pointed teeth, and dripped slowly down her chin.

"Ugh!" gasped the queue of children.

"Gross!" shuddered Lauren.

"Puts you off hamburgers, doesn't it?" grinned her brother.

"I wonder where Daniel and Holly are," said Lauren, looking around. Daniel and Holly were school friends.

"They said they'd be by the Hall of Mirrors," said James. "Hang on while I tell Mum and Dad where we are, then we'll see if they've arrived."

When they got to the Hall of Mirrors Daniel and Holly were waiting.

"Shall we go in here first?" asked Holly.

"Yes, let's!" said Lauren.

"Then we'll give the ghost train a go," said Daniel.

"It's supposed to be really scary," said Holly.

"Says who?" scoffed James. "What's a few cobwebs brushing against your face?"

"And a white sheet flapping and moaning," added Daniel.

"It's all fake, anyway," said James.

"How do you know?" asked Lauren.

"Because there are no such things as ghosts," said Daniel. "Everyone knows that."

The Hall of Mirrors was silly, and stupid, and good fun. The distorted mirrors made everyone look like freaks. James told Holly she looked better with a head the size of a pin and a huge bottom, and Holly called him a stick insect when she saw his matchstick reflection. Secretly she thought the name suited him. James was quite tall and thin in real life.

"Look at us!" called Lauren and Daniel. Lauren had a neck like an ostrich and Daniel was as round as a hippopotamus.

"Tweedle-dum and Tweedle-dee," laughed Holly.

The two girls turned to look at a woman standing next to them. She was very short, and was wearing a fussy brown coat. On her head she wore a red hat with a feather in it. In the distorted mirror her reflection looked like a mad chicken.

Daniel made a clucking noise. It was too much for the girls. They started to giggle, and once they'd started they couldn't stop. Then Lauren gave an enormous snort. Putting their hands over their mouths the two of them dashed for the exit.

"What's got into you?" asked Lauren's

dad when he saw them laughing outside.

"Go in and you'll see for yourself," gasped Holly, holding on to her friend.

"Silly children," smiled Lauren's mother. It always made her smile when the children were happy.

"Brains the size of a chicken's," said Dad.

This made the girls laugh even more.

When they arrived at the ghost train, it had just left for a trip into the haunted house. The children gathered around the notice outside.

THE SCARIEST TRAIN RIDE EVER!
GHOSTS AND GHOULS!
BATS AND SPIDERS!
SEE THE DEMON WITH EYES LIKE BURNING COALS.
WHEN HE LAUGHS, FEEL YOUR BLOOD RUN COLD!

MEET THE GHOST WHO DANCES NIGHT AND DAY.
PITY THE DROWNING GHOST AS SHE DISAPPEARS UNDER THE WATER.
ENTER THE HAUNTED HOUSE AT YOUR PERIL.
YOU WILL NEVER BE THE SAME AGAIN!!

The children looked at each other.

"Sounds scary," said Lauren.

"It will be pathetic," said Daniel. "A few fake cobwebs touching your face. A few pretend ghosts shrieking and moaning. It'll be nothing."

"Hmmm," said Holly. She wasn't so sure. The ghost train had just returned and she had seen the faces of the passengers. Nobody was smiling. One little boy was crying.

"Do you want the first carriage?" the

attendant asked when they got on board.

"Yes, please," said the children. It's always scarier in the first carriage.

When the ghost train entered the haunted house everything seemed perfectly normal. There was a brightly lit hallway and a friendly, cheerful-looking kitchen. A family of four was sitting around a table talking and laughing. Dad was eating a bowl of cereal and Mum was buttering a piece of toast. A little dog was sitting watching them. The smallest girl gave him a piece of her toast.

"Hannah, don't feed Rusty at the table," said Dad.

"OK," said Hannah.

The dog moved to where another girl was sitting, in the hope that she would feed him.

"No way," said the girl. But the dog sat waiting anyway.

The four children looked at this domestic scene in surprise. It was a bit like a programme on TV.

Then the train moved from the kitchen into a sitting-room. Here two boys were watching television. There was a fire burning in the hearth and the lamps were lit. It looked very cosy.

"This is boring," said Daniel.

"When is the fun going to start?" wondered Lauren.

"We want fun!" chanted James. "We want fun!"

"What's that smell?" asked Holly, holding her nose.

As she spoke, the fire in the hearth

died, and the air became very cold. There was a strong smell of rotting vegetables. Then the lamps went out and the room became pitch black.

Someone, or something, started to laugh. It was a loud laugh, loud and harsh and humourless. It was the sort of laugh that made you shiver.

Lauren clutched Holly's hand. The laughter got louder, and in the darkness the children could see what looked like two burning coals high up above their heads. The burning coals came closer and closer, until the children could see they were crimson eye sockets in a skull. The ghostly skull hovered in front of them, staring with blood-red eyes, then Holly felt the touch of icy fingers on her cheek.

Her scream filled the empty darkness, and was almost as frightening as the horrible laughter.

Then the lamps came on again. The fire in the hearth re-lit and the two boys continued to watch television. The children could see the flickering of the TV screen. Suddenly, everything was back to normal.

Then they heard music – sad, haunting music. And against the backdrop of the dark curtains a ghost appeared and began to dance. "One, two, three...one, two, three..." Arms outstretched, it waltzed round and round the room, twirling and spinning. "One, two, three...one, two, three...one, two, three...one, two, three." As it passed close to them the children could see its feet were bandaged.

"Is this the ghost that never stops dancing?" whispered Lauren.

"I suppose it must be," muttered James.

The train entered a dimly lit passage. Cobwebs hung from the ceiling, trailing sticky strands of gossamer in the children's faces, and spiders with gross hairy legs landed on them. Bats flew around their heads, and giant moths tangled in their hair.

The two boys were beginning to enjoy themselves.

"This is more like it," said James.

"Spooky," agreed Daniel.

The two girls didn't say anything.

The train had come to a halt. They were in what looked like a cellar. The walls were damp and dripping, and the front of the train was almost submerged in a pool of dark, still water.

If the children had felt scared before, it was nothing to what they felt now. They heard a soft, slurping sound, and the surface of the water was disturbed by a swirl of ripples.

Then, a head emerged!

It was the head of a woman. The children could see her long hair floating around her face. The woman gave a gasp and a small cry. "Help me," she called to the children. "Help me, please." Then she disappeared again beneath the surface...

When the train came out of the haunted house into the bright daylight, the children were silent.

"That was horrible," said Lauren, at last.

"I'm not going in there again," said Holly. "I've never been so scared in all my life."

"You were meant to be scared," said James. "That's the point of it."

"It seemed so real," said Lauren.

"Of course it seemed real," James grinned, "but it's all fake, honestly."

"I bet if we went in again we would spot what tricks they used," said Daniel.

"You can't possibly go in again," said Holly, horrified.

"Want a bet?" James replied.

While Daniel and James were in the haunted house for the second time the girls wandered off to a nearby stall, which was selling stuff for Halloween. Two witches were behind the counter stirring a huge cauldron.

"Write a number on a piece of paper and put it in the cauldron," said one of the witches. "If we pick it out, this book of magic will be yours." And she burst into loud, cackling laughter.

"Think of a number," said Lauren to Holly.

Holly wrote '1020', then dropped the paper into the pot. The two witches began to stir vigorously while chanting...

"Eye of toad and hair of bat,

Tooth of dog and toe of rat,

Mix together in a stew

And pick a number just for you."

Putting her hand in the pot, one of the witches drew out a slip of paper. She showed it to the girls. On it was written the number 75.

Disappointed, the girls turned to leave.

"Wait, my pretties," whined the witch, "we haven't finished yet. You think of a spell, and try again."

Holly thought hard, then said...

"Tittle-tattle, tittle-tattle

I am ready for this battle,

Stir a little, stir a lot,

And pick my number from this pot."

The witch put her hand in the

cauldron and drew out another slip of paper.

"1020," she shrieked, jumping up and down.

"That's it!" shouted the girls. "That's the number."

Grumbling and complaining, the witches gave Holly the book of magic and, putting it in her pocket, she and Lauren made their way back to the haunted house.

When they arrived the train was just emerging from the tunnel. It was packed with people. The girls looked carefully at the faces, searching for the two boys.

But they were nowhere to be seen!

"Funny," said Lauren. "Where can they be?"

"Perhaps they didn't go in, after all," said Holly.

"But we saw them!" said Lauren. "They were definitely on the train."

"I'll go in on the next ride," said the attendant when he saw how worried the girls were. "If there is anything wrong, I'll put it right, don't you fret."

"They couldn't get off the train, could they?" Holly asked him. "While it was inside the haunted house?"

"They could," said the attendant, "but they'd be pretty stupid if they did."

"Why would they get off?" asked Lauren, looking at her friend.

"I haven't a clue," said Holly, shaking her head.

When the attendant emerged from the haunted house, he was frowning.

"No," he said in answer to the girls'

questions, "I didn't see any sign of them. But..."

"But what?" Lauren interrupted, anxiously.

"Something's not right. The dancing ghost didn't show up, for a start."

"Has something broken down?" asked Lauren.

"If it has, I can't fix it now," said the attendant. "I'll do it later when we close for the night."

"Shall we go in again?" Lauren asked her friend, when the attendant had left them.

"I don't know!" said Holly. The haunted house had really scared her.

"There's no point in hanging about here," said Lauren. "Let's go in and see for ourselves. If the boys are definitely not in there, we'll tell Mum and Dad. They'll know what to do."

When the ghost train entered the haunted house again, everything seemed pretty much as it had before. The family in the kitchen was still eating breakfast. The girls could see the little dog, still waiting for titbits under the table. It was the same in the living room. The fire was burning in the hearth. The lamps were lit and the two boys were watching television. They had their backs to the girls.

Then one boy moved his head. And when he did, Lauren had the shock of her life.

It was her brother, James!

Lauren didn't know whether to feel relieved or afraid. Then the other boy moved and she could see that it was Daniel.

"It's them," she whispered to Holly.

"What shall we do?" Holly whispered back.

"Let's call them," said Lauren.

At first they called quietly, but when the boys didn't answer they tried calling louder...and louder...until in the end they were shouting.

But the boys didn't hear them!

Then the lamp went out as it had before, and the fire died. The air went cold, and there was the same smell of rotting vegetables. The girls looked up as the ghost with the burning eyes hovered above them. This time it was silent, and somehow the silence was worse than the laughter they had heard before. Closer and closer it came until it was right above them. Then it beckoned to the girls with a long, bony finger...

"What does it want?" whispered Lauren.

"Come with me," sighed the ghost. "Come with me."

As soon as they heard the ghost speak the girls no longer felt afraid. They stepped out of the train into a cloud of white mist and felt themselves floating upwards. When the mist cleared they were in a large, sunny room where the boys were waiting for them.

Lauren hugged her brother.

"Steady on," he grinned, hugging her back.

"We were so worried," she said.

"We hoped you would look for us," said Daniel, "because without you we can't help our new friends."

"Which new friends?" Lauren asked.

"Boris, Ronald and Rowena," answered Daniel. "They're ghosts!"

"You're kidding?"

"No, honestly, it's true." James began to explain. "Poor Boris, Ronald and Rowena are trapped here, in the haunted house, against their will. Unless we help them they'll probably stay forever."

"Which one's Boris?" asked Holly.

"He's the ghost that brought you here," said James. "Ronald is the dancing one..."

"...and poor Rowena is the ghost who was drowning," finished Daniel.

"How can we help?" asked Lauren.

"We have to get hold of a book of magic. In it is a spell which will set the ghosts free, but it must be read out by a young female...a girl."

"That's weird," said Lauren. "Holly's just won a book of magic."

Holly handed her book to James, who

flicked through and began to read:

"Bring me something nice for tea,
Like jellyfish, fresh from the sea.
And juicy worms and fat white slugs
Cooked with spiders, bats and bugs.
Obey me now or you will find
A tail will grow on your behind."

"That doesn't sound at all right," said Lauren.

"Give it to me," said Holly, and taking the book she started to look through it. The others watched and waited. Suddenly, Holly burst out, "This could be the one!

"Spirits trapped in this strange place
Longing to be free to roam,
Come and look into my face
Then you can start your journey home."

"That's more like it," said Lauren.

"Let's give it a try," said James.

He called the ghosts into the room.

"This is my sister Lauren and her

friend Holly," he explained to the ghosts.

"We know," sighed Boris, his eyes burning, "we've already met."

"Have you got the book of magic?" asked Ronald.

"Yes," said Holly, holding it up. Now she was face-to-face with the ghosts she didn't feel at all afraid. She began to read:

"Spirits trapped in this strange place
Longing to be free to roam,
Come and look into my face
Then you can start your journey home."

As she read she gazed at the ghosts. When she had finished she reached out to touch them, but it was like putting her hand into a cloud – there was nothing there.

"Thank you, all of you," said Ronald.

"Thank you," said Boris.

"You've been so kind," said Rowena.

And then, suddenly, the cloud-like mist disappeared.

"Where have you been?" the attendant asked James and Daniel, when they walked out of the tunnel. "You must never get out of the train when it is in the haunted house!"

"We won't," said the children, relieved that he hadn't asked any more questions.

That afternoon the attendant had complaints from all his customers.

"This ghost train is boring," said one.

"What's the point of a ghost train if there are no ghosts?" said another.

"I wanted to see the drowning ghost," said a boy with pimples.

The attendant looked at them as if

they were mad. "What are they talking about?" he thought.

But that evening, when he went to look for himself, he had a big surprise. His customers were right. There were no ghosts!

The haunted house was quiet and empty. It seemed like an ordinary house.

The only thing the attendant found that was a bit odd was a little book of magic. It was lying on a table in the room at the top of the house. Inside was a slip of paper that said...

"We have gone far away
To a land where spirits long to be.
A land of colour, warmth and light,
Where we can wander and be free."

And it was signed...Boris, Ronald and Rowena.

The Polite Pirate

The ship's passengers were just settling themselves on deck for the afternoon. The ship had been sailing for over a week now and everyone, even the crew, was surprised by how mild the weather had been. A few of the older passengers were sunbathing and chatting together. They heard the cry first.

"PIRATES!"

The cry spread like wildfire. It was passed on from one end of the ship to the other. "Pirates!" someone would say in a hushed voice to the person next to him, who would repeat it to his neighbour until the entire ship was running around in a panic.

The passengers ran here, there and

everywhere, but no one seemed to know where to go or what to do. And the crew were no help. They were just as terrified as everyone else.

Then there was another shout. "There they are, it's them!" And they could see the first pirates who were about to board the ship.

Most of the pirates looked as everyone expected them to look – unkempt, swarthy, vicious and as if they would just as soon cut your throat as look at you.

Except for one, who must have been the captain. He was tall and well dressed and looked more like an officer than a pirate. He wore a tightly fitted jacket made of burgundy velvet and a black felt hat with a peacock-blue feather sticking out. He looked down on all the hurrying and scurrying and shouting, and put up his hand for silence. At this command everything stopped and the entire ship went quiet.

"Ladies and gentlemen," he said in a surprisingly pleasant voice, "I'm very sorry for this inconvenience, which I can assure you won't last very long. But in the meantime I would be grateful if you would take out your wallets and remove your jewellery."

Then he very calmly walked over to each passenger, with his elegant hat held out, and he waited patiently while they passed over their valuables. And, as each person handed over rings and money, he would thank them. "Thank you so much," he said. "I'm sorry to trouble you." And once or twice he even added, "I hope you enjoy the rest of your voyage."

Now, although people don't like to be robbed, the pirate captain did it with such charm that they didn't mind as much as they normally would have.

When he reached an old woman called Mrs Williams, he placed his hat in front of her, just as he had done with the other passengers. She hesitated over her diamond ring and said, "Oh, but this ring means so much to me. You see…" and tears welled in her eyes, "it belonged to my beloved grandmother, who gave it to me when she was on her deathbed…and…"

But the pirate captain quickly stopped her. "I understand," he said. "I know what it's like when things have a sentimental value. Keep it, dear lady, with my compliments."

When they heard this, his fellow

pirates weren't too happy. "But them's diamonds," scowled one of them, who had a bright-red scar on his left cheek. But his captain just glared at him.

"Oh, thank you so much," Mrs Williams said. "I'm so grateful."

The other passengers noted what had happened and, when it was their turn, they all came out with different stories. One said his mother was sick and he needed his money to look after her. Another said that he'd just lost his job and was hoping to find work in another country.

The pirate captain listened to them all and was so moved by their stories that he let them keep their valuables. And he even handed a few coins to an old man who looked particularly shabbily dressed.

Then he said goodbye to everyone and again wished them all a good journey, and he and the other pirates left the ship.

When the passengers were sure that he and his pirates had left, they all breathed a sigh of relief.

"What a nice chap," one of them said.

"Yes, very polite," everyone agreed. "Probably the most polite pirate we'll ever see."

But just who was this pirate captain who was so polite?

His name was Pemberton Hardy the Third. But other than his name, not much was known about him, although there were certainly enough rumours. Some said he was the son of a rich banker who had been kidnapped by pirates. Others thought that he was the son of an earl who had fallen in love with a farmer's daughter. When his father forced him to stop seeing her, he was so broken-hearted that he ran away to sea.

Everyone who met Captain Pemberton found him fascinating. But the only people who didn't fall under his spell were the pirates who served under him. They couldn't understand why he was so polite, or why he was so generous.

A few weeks later, Captain Pemberton was sitting in his cabin writing a letter. Suddenly his first mate, Scowling Sid, came rushing in, saying that he'd spotted a perfect ship for plundering.

"Proceed at full speed," the captain replied.

He quickly buckled his sword, put on his hat and strode out on deck. As soon as the other ship was near enough, he got ready to jump aboard. But then he noticed that another pirate ship had come alongside with the same idea. He turned to face the other pirate captain.

"After you," he said.

"But you were here first," said the other captain, who was a fair man.

"But I insist," said Pemberton.

"No, you go first," said the other captain, who suspected it may be a trap.

"No, I insist," Pemberton replied.

They were so busy being polite that neither realized that while they were having their polite discussion, the crew and passengers of the ship they were about to plunder had very quietly lowered the rowboats. Quickly and quietly, they were all rowing away from their boat.

This left the two captains looking slightly confused, while their crews looked on in disbelief.

"I can't believe you let them get away," snorted Snarling Sam, the head mate with only one eye.

"There were some good pickings there," added Big John Copper, who was almost two metres tall.

"And the only reason we lost it," snapped Scowling Sid, "was because of you and your stupid manners."

"That's right," Moody Roger chimed in. "We're tired of you and your good manners. We're pirates, not boy scouts!"

Pemberton had heard the men complain before, but never like this. He knew he would have to put a stop to it quickly.

"We may be pirates," he said, "but that doesn't mean we have to be hairy cut-throats with the manners of gorillas. We don't do it just for treasure. What about the adventure! The excitement! Meeting new people!"

But the rest of the pirates weren't very impressed.

"What new people?" Snarling Sam asked. "We only meet them long enough to rob them, and then we forget them. It's not as if we're going to call in for tea when we're next in port. But, if we're going to rob them, then let's do it right. Let's take what they've got, and make no bones about it."

All the other pirates shouted in agreement.

Pemberton could see that things were getting serious.

"Why don't we discuss it after tea," he said.

"That's another thing," shouted Big John Copper. "Other pirates drink rum."

"Straight out of the bottle," added Moody Roger. "And what do we get? Tea! That's not being a real pirate. You can't sing 'Yo-ho-ho, and a cup of tea!' It doesn't sound right."

By this time the pirates were getting

very hot and bothered. They had worked themselves into such a state that they were losing their tempers. They had become an angry mob. And this mob was heading for mutiny.

It was hard to tell how it actually began. Or who started it off. That's the way it is with mutinies. Someone grabbed Pemberton from behind and, as he was turning around to see who it was, someone else hit him from the front. And the next thing he knew he was thrown into a very smelly, cold, damp room. He was a prisoner in the hold of his own ship.

Once the captain was out of the way, Snarling Sam and Scowling Sid brought out a bottle of rum that they had been hiding in their bunks. Snarling Sam raised the bottle high.

"Tea will be a little on the strong side this afternoon," he snarled. And, as

everybody cheered, he took a big swig, then passed the bottle around to the other pirates until it finally reached Big John Copper. By this time the bottle was empty, which didn't make him too happy. But they all felt like real pirates now. So when Scowling Sid and Snarling Sam announced that they were now in charge of the ship, nobody argued.

The first thing they did was change the name of the ship from *The Courteous Rogue* to *The Mean Bandit*.

"Now we'll show them what kind of pirates we really are," announced the new captain and first mate. And they meant it.

To make up for lost time, the ship went on a mad spree of looting and robbing. They scoured the high seas shouting, "Your money or your life," brandishing their gleaming swords, their rotten teeth and their eye patches.

Soon, no ship felt safe from the clutches of *The Mean Bandit*. When they saw a French vessel that was full of wine, they lost no time in emptying it. They did the same to a Dutch cargo ship that was full of biscuits. It didn't matter what the cargo was. If it was useful or valuable, they took it on board. If it wasn't, they dumped it into the sea, laughing.

The final straw came when the pirates of *The Mean Bandit* raided a Spanish ship. The King of Spain himself just happened to be travelling on this particular ship. The pirates lost no time in ransacking the ship.

Snarling Sam not only made the King hand over his coins and his pocket watch, but demanded his crown as well.

Scowling Sid took a fancy to the King's boots. The boots were made of gleaming Spanish leather, and the King wore the same shoe size as Scowling Sid.

Then the pirates realized that the King would fetch a large royal ransom. So they threw him into the hold with Pemberton.

The Spanish government immediately complained to the Queen of England. She called in the Admiral of the Fleet and began telling him about the complaints she had been receiving. The Admiral listened politely but didn't seem surprised.

"I have heard similar stories, Your Majesty," he said. "They say even other pirate ships are becoming afraid of this vessel."

"Something must be done!" demanded

the Queen.

"Leave it to me, Your Majesty," the Admiral said. Then he went home to work out a plan.

On board the pirate ship, meanwhile, most of the crew were asleep in their bunks. Only the nightwatch man was awake. Big John Copper liked the night watch. On a good night, with a few tots of rum after a good meal, he could see mermaids. In fact, he was looking at one right now. He had spotted her just a little while ago, just after his last swig of rum. In fact, if he stared hard, he thought he could see two identical mermaids.

Big John Copper was so busy looking for mermaids that he didn't see the two rowboats very quietly pull up beside the ship. He didn't spot the twenty sailors, led by the Admiral himself, who silently climbed aboard ***The Mean Bandit***. And when he finally turned around it was too late. One of the sailors was right behind him. One clean blow on his head did the trick. And, after that, all he saw was stars.

Once Big John was out of the way, the rest was easy. The sailors tiptoed to the bunks and, before the pirates knew what was happening, they were tied up. A few, like Scowling Sid, did manage to rush out of bed and grab their swords. But in the darkness they couldn't see what they were doing and ended up fighting each other.

It didn't take long for the sailors to round up the entire crew. The Admiral's plan had worked perfectly. The pirates were brought out in twos. The Admiral congratulated his men on a job well done. Then he turned to two of the sailors and said, "Go and look in the hold and see if there are any prisoners."

Soon they came back with Pemberton and the King of Spain. Pemberton looked much thinner. His uniform was dishevelled and it was obvious that he hadn't shaved for some time. But he still managed to look elegant. The King had been in the hold for a short time, but was still barefoot and, for some reason, looked a lot worse.

They brought the two men to the middle of the deck. The Admiral addressed Pemberton first. "What's your name?" he asked.

"Pemberton Hardy the Third," he replied.

"And what's your connection with this ship?"

"I, Sir," Pemberton answered grandly,

"am the captain of this ship."

"He doesn't look like a pirate," one of the sailors said.

"And he certainly doesn't sound like one," his mate added.

The Admiral continued the questioning. "And what's the name of your ship?"

If Pemberton was surprised to be asked what seemed like a silly question, he didn't show it.

"***The Courteous Rogue,***" he answered, and all the sailors burst out laughing.

"We had better let him go," the Admiral said. "He's harmless enough. All that time in the cell must have made his mind go a little funny."

Then he turned to the King. "And you sir, pray tell, what is your name?"

"I am Juan Carlos," he said in a very thick Spanish accent, "King of Spain."

Suddenly the Admiral remembered having heard from the Queen that there was a royal prisoner from Spain. He quickly looked through the papers she had given him, which he had in his coat pocket. Among them was a document with the King's signature. He drew out another sheet and took out a pen, which he gave to the King.

"Your Majesty," said the Admiral, "would you mind writing your signature?"

"It would give me great pleasure," the King said, and signed his name with a flourish, as if he was signing an important document.

The Admiral compared both signatures, and sure enough they matched. Then, removing his hat, he gave a low bow and said, "This is proof, Your Majesty, that you really are the King. Please accept the humble apologies of the Queen of England

and me for the way you have been treated."

The King graciously accepted the apology and then told the Admiral about how his boots were taken, and his crown. A search party was immediately dispatched and all the items were found. The boots, which were still on Scowling Sid's feet, were quickly removed.

When the King had put his boots back on, the Admiral asked him, "Your Majesty, is there anything we can do to make amends for the terrible way you have been treated?"

"Just one little favour, if you don't mind," the King said. "That funny fellow, the one who was in the cell with me, what is his name?...Oh, yes, Pemberton. Would you mind if he came back with me to Spain?"

"Your Majesty, you have yourself a companion."

The Admiral and his sailors took over the ship and headed for the closest port. Then all the pirates were arrested and sent to prison for a good long time. And Pemberton and the King of Spain were put on a separate boat that was heading for Spain.

Once they were in Spain, the King, who had become good friends with Pemberton, made him Admiral of the Spanish fleet and gave him the command of the largest ship in the Spanish navy.

I Was the World's Worst Astronaut

Do you know much about space? For instance, do you think there might be aliens living on other planets, and what do you think it would be like to stand on the moon? There are heaps of things I don't know about space, but I can answer those two questions for you.

My name's Fred. By the way, I'm a cleaner. I work at Mission Control, a place where space rockets get launched to the moon. Did you know that space rockets gradually fill up with rubbish left behind by untidy astronauts, just like cars fill up with sweet wrappers dropped by children (not by you, of course)? I really love my job, which is to clean out the rockets ready for their next mission. It makes me proud to think they leave Earth sparkling and smelling of my lemon cleaning liquid.

Cleaning is what I do best, but one day that all changed. I was on my way home when I noticed an empty rocket standing on the launchpad. I always carry my best feather duster with me, for good luck, so I thought I'd use it.

"I'll just tidy that one up," I thought to myself and I climbed inside. I vacuumed the floor, flicked my duster around, and then I picked up a couple of old spaceboots and socks left behind by those messy astronauts. Out of the corner of my eye I saw a spacesuit hanging up in the corner. I couldn't resist trying it on. At first I just slipped one arm into it. Then, before I could stop myself, I tried on the whole outfit, helmet and all!

"Moon, here I come!" I cried, pointing

my feather duster up into space and pretending to be a real astronaut, just for fun. I took a big step forward but, because I wasn't used to wearing the helmet I toppled over my own feet. I'm ashamed to say I landed on the main control panel and accidentally pressed a big red button with my elbow.

The button started to flash. There was a roar, and the floor shook. I saw flames billow out of the rocket engines outside the window. I was scared, I can tell you, especially when I was thrown back into one of the rocket seats and straps sprang out to pin me down. My helmet had a two-way radio on the side, and it crackled into life.

"Ground Control to Rocket One. It's a bit early to launch, but now you've started the engines you'll have to carry on. You're clear for take-off. Ten. Nine. Eight..."

Someone began to count down loudly

in my ear.

"Please stop!" I begged.

"Seven. Six. Five..." the voice carried on.

"Can you please stop counting?" I cried, but the voice just carried on:

"Four. Three. Two. One...Blast off!"

"I'm not an astronaut! I'm a cleaner!" I shouted. But my words were drowned out by the screaming engines as the rocket shot into the air at hundreds of kilometres an hour.

I screwed my eyes tightly shut and hoped I was only in a horrible dream that would go away when I woke up. But when I dared to open them again it was worse

than ever. Through the rocket window I could see Earth far away. It looked like a beach ball, hanging in a sky as black as ink.

My helmet radio clicked on again.

"Come in, come in, Rocket One. This is Frank at Mission Control on Earth. Are you receiving me? Hello? For goodness sake, press the green button on your helmet so I can hear you. What kind of astronaut forgets that?"

I pressed the button and mumbled into the radio microphone.

"I'm not an astronaut. I'm Fred the cleaner."

"You're WHAT?" the person called Frank yelled, and I was glad for a moment that I was in space and not in the same room as him. He was shouting the rudest words I've ever heard!

I didn't much want to hear somebody else panicking. I was feeling bad enough already. I decided to make a cup of coffee to settle my nerves so I unstrapped myself from my seat, but then I had my next big shock. Instead of standing up, I floated up! I found out that, in space, people are weightless and float about like balloons. It was a very weird feeling. I kept bumping into the sides of the rocket. But then I worked out a way of swimming through the air, and after a while I even did a somersault.

Frank from Mission Control spoilt the fun by shouting into my ear through the helmet radio.

"Hello! Hello! Are you receiving me?"

I was just starting a somersault and he made me jump, so I messed it up and bruised my bum on the ceiling. I was glad he'd called, though, because I needed to ask him an urgent question.

"Hello...um...can you tell me where

the toilet is on this rocket?" I asked. There was a silence, then Frank replied.

"Do you have any astronaut training at all?" he asked, and I could hear his voice was a bit shaky.

"Nope," I replied.

"Listen, buddy. You're on your way to the moon. I don't know how it happened but we're going to have to make the best of it," he explained. Then I heard his big sigh whistle through the microphone.

"OK, but can you hurry up and tell me where the toilet is?" I asked. It's hard to cross your legs when you're floating.

Frank tried to explain to me how to use the built-in rocket toilet. Remember, everything floats around in a rocket – and I mean everything. So the toilet had been designed by the world's brainiest scientists to stop that happening, but I can tell you it was the most uncomfortable toilet ever.

Astronauts have to put up with a lot.

After that I floated around the rocket for a while, doing a spot of cleaning to make me feel more at home.

"Are you hungry?" Frank asked me through the radio. He told me where the food cupboard was and I had high hopes of finding doughnuts and burgers. But there was nothing like that, only lots of packets strapped inside the cupboard to stop them floating off. On the side of each packet there was a straw.

"That's your space food. You have to suck it out of the packet because if you put it on a plate it would float away," Frank explained.

I tried one that was

labelled 'soup', but it tasted just like cardboard. Then I tried one marked 'stew', which tasted of bathroom sponge. I accidentally split the packet marked 'custard' and a string of yellow blobs floated off around the rocket in a sort of custard storm.

"Oops, I spilt my pudding," I told Frank. He didn't reply to me but I heard him whispering to someone else, "Wow, that guy is stupid."

Well, I'd like to see him try to catch custard blobs in his mouth while swimming through the air. Actually, I was pretty good at it. Unfortunately, I did knock into one or two important-looking controls while I was trying and the rocket started to make a rattling noise like my old car at home. I noticed lots of alarm lights flashing, too. I thought I'd better tell Frank.

"You're going to have to go outside to

repair the heating system. Otherwise you're soon going to be frozen solid like a lollipop," Frank announced.

I didn't fancy being a lollipop.

"I'll just open the door, then," I said, but Frank started yelling.

"NO! You have to put on your full spacesuit, helmet, gloves, boots and everything. Otherwise as soon as you get outside you'll fry and explode at the same time," he warned.

I didn't really believe you could do both at the same time, but Frank insisted you could. He said it was very complicated to explain why and he didn't really have the time. He said I had to do exactly what he said, and nothing else.

He told me how to open the rocket doors properly. Finally, after a lot of fiddling about, I stepped out into space. A long cord attached to the rocket kept me from floating away. I must have looked like a fish on the end of a line but, luckily, there was nobody around to laugh at me. It was very quiet out there, and dark too. I could still see Earth but it was tiny now, like a blue paint splodge on a black cloth that was stretched over everything.

I floated gently over to the side of the rocket and, at first, I did exactly what Frank told me to do through the radio. Holding on to the side of the rocket with one hand, I tightened a few screws and turned a few handles with the other.

"You're doing a good job, Fred. Now go back inside," Frank congratulated me. But I couldn't resist giving the rocket a little clean with my best feather duster, which I had sneaked outside in my pocket without telling him, just to bring me good luck.

This was a big mistake. I reached up high to dust the top of the rocket and lost

my grip. I floated away from the rocket and began to spin around on the end of the cord. It started to tangle up in a big knot. I think it very nearly broke!

"Frank! Help!" I shouted, dropping my precious best feather duster.

"Grab on to something, quick, before you float away!" Frank shouted.

I reached for the door of the rocket and just managed to get my fingers around it. Then I crept inside, feeling very silly and dizzy, too. I watched sadly through the rocket window as my best feather duster floated off into outer space. I hope it finds a good home on a planet where they love cleaning as much as I do.

I was very tired, so I told Frank I needed a rest. I knew it wouldn't be simple. I had to strap myself into a bed so I wouldn't float around. Even more weird, the bed was on the wall, so I had to sleep standing up. It's all so complicated living in space.

When I fell asleep I dreamed about the world's cleanest planet where my best feather duster was crowned king, and litter was banned forever, especially sweet papers and empty juice cartons. I wouldn't mind going into space again, and putting up with the odd beds and toilets, if I could visit such a wonderful place.

A few hours later I was woken up by Frank on the radio.

"Wakey, wakey! It's a lovely day here on Earth and an exciting day for you, Fred. You're going to land on the moon and do some rock collecting," he explained.

I didn't like the thought of that job at all. It sounded messy. Then I looked out of the window and got quite a surprise. The Moon was really close and getting closer all the time. It was dusty and covered in lumps of rock, which made it look very untidy.

"Stay strapped in. The rocket is going to land automatically," Frank explained. I heard the engines make a different noise. The rocket swung around and sank down, bumping gently onto the ground.

"Fred, you have to go outside again. Pick up some stones and then come straight back in quickly. Do you understand?" Frank asked. He sounded as if he thought I was really stupid, so I didn't bother to answer him. In fact he made me so grumpy I switched the helmet radio off.

I put on all my equipment and opened the rocket doors again. This time I took my second-best feather duster with me. I didn't care what Frank said about being quick. I could see the moon needed a good clean and I was going to do my bit to make it shine. I did collect some of his boring stones, too.

It all took a while but nothing went wrong, or so I thought. When I switched my helmet radio back on Frank shouted at me for not keeping in contact, but I told him not to fuss.

I carried his dull old stones back to the rocket, pleased with my cleaning work. But when I got back inside and took my helmet off I got the fright of my life. I hadn't shut the door properly, you see. Something had climbed in and was now sitting in my seat. When it saw me it spoke.

"Splidge, splidge."

I guessed it was an alien from the moon. It had a big fat head like a pumpkin, bulgy purple eyes like gobstoppers and lots of rainbow-coloured spots. It also had fourteen waving wiggling arms and five mouths.

"Hey, what's going on?" Frank's voice came out of the helmet radio suddenly and made the alien jump. It grabbed the helmet, opened one of its five mouths and swallowed it whole! I could hear Frank's voice coming from somewhere inside it. When the alien opened its mouth and burped, I clearly heard Frank say, "What?"

At first I felt scared, but the alien waved all its arms and smiled with all its mouths, and looked friendly, so I thought we should try to make friends.

"My name's

Fred," I introduced myself.

"Splidge," the alien replied, then it pointed out of the window towards Earth.

"Do you want to go there?" I asked, and the alien waved its arms wildly.

"The only problem is, I don't know how to work this rocket, and Frank (the one who does) is on the end of a radio inside your tummy," I explained.

"Splidge, splidge," the alien replied, and began pushing some of the rocket buttons with his funny three-fingered hands. The rocket zoomed up from the moon and pointed itself towards Earth. That's when I realized that, unlike me, the alien was a really good astronaut! After that we got on fine. I called him Splidge because that's the word he said most. I offered him some food packets, which he swallowed whole, straw and all. Then we floated around the rocket and I showed him how to do somersaults. Meanwhile Earth got bigger and bigger outside the window. We were on our way home.

"I hope the other humans won't mind me bringing a friend to visit," I remarked as Splidge landed our rocket expertly back at Mission Control. I was looking forward to introducing Splidge to everyone.

Things didn't go smoothly straight away, though. There was a crowd of official-looking people waiting for us when we stepped out of the rocket, but they didn't cheer. When they saw Splidge they gasped and we were hurried away to a secret location. I had to make a speech explaining to them that Splidge was not going to eat them all, or take over the world. All he wanted to do was to have a nice holiday on Earth.

Eventually, they realized that Splidge was harmless and very clever. They agreed to let him stay. As well as controlling rockets, he turned out to be very good at mending anything small and fiddly, so he was a great help to everyone. He even offered to do my cleaning job. With so many arms he could finish it much faster than me. I thanked him for the kind offer but I said I'd rather do it myself because I loved it so much.

I finally got to meet Frank, the man who had spoken to me on my helmet radio while I was on my space adventure. He had snow-white hair. Apparently it had been brown, but it had turned white overnight when he realized that I was on board his rocket and I couldn't even suck custard through a straw without making a mistake.

A day or two later the Prime Minister himself visited Mission Control to meet me and Splidge. He gave us both medals, and then got Splidge to mend his old watch. He

offered me a job advising him on aliens, but I said no. I love cleaning, you see. I don't want to do anything else.

So I got my old job back and I now wander around Mission Control, polishing the doorknobs and picking up the sweet wrappers. I don't ever want to travel in a rocket again, but I'm very proud because I know I've had a big effect on space, one that all of you can see.

All you have to do is look at the moon, on nights when it's big and round. I am certain that it shines brighter because I cleaned it when I was there.

William and the Tiniest Dragon

William didn't believe anything he was told. He was a boy who always had to see for himself. He was also a pretty clever boy. Even when he was a toddler, he realized that grown ups say some very silly things to children.

When his mother wanted him to eat up his dinner, she used to play games. William thought that was very silly.

"Here comes the big orange plane," Mum would coo. "Coming in to land at Mouth Airport!" Then she would swoop a large spoonful of carrots towards his mouth.

William would look at her with a big frown. "It isn't," he would say, and then shut his mouth firmly.

When William tried out his new plastic hammer on Mr Bear's nose, his father tried to stop him. "Oh William! You're hurting poor Mr Bear," Dad said. "He'll be upset."

"He isn't alive, you know," said William coldly.

When William was older, things became even more difficult. He got into lots of trouble at Grandma's birthday party. Grandma giggled and told everyone that she was 39. When William said, "You've got to be joking!" in a very loud voice, Grandma got rather upset. And William was sent to his room.

William's teacher thought he was hard work. He always wanted her to prove anything she said. Sometimes that could be difficult.

"The moon is very different from

Earth," said Mrs Martin. "Nobody lives there and nothing grows there."

All the children in the class wrote what she said in their books. All except William.

"How do you know there's nothing growing on the moon?" asked William. "Have you ever been there?"

"No, of course not," replied the teacher, "but other people have. Their reports say that there is nothing at all growing on the moon. So that's how we know."

"People often don't tell the truth," said William. "How do you know you can trust them?"

"You'll just have to take my word for it, William," Mrs Martin replied. "Now we must move on."

She knew that William's questions could take up the whole lesson. It was very difficult.

There were not many subjects that William felt happy about. Maths was fine. He could work out all the problems and see for himself that everything was true. He could prove it. Music was OK, too. He could hear with his own ears if something sounded right.

History, on the other hand, was very difficult. How could he be sure that the history books were telling the truth? How could anyone know for certain what happened hundreds of years ago? Geography was just as bad. How could he be sure that the maps were *right*? How did anyone know what the centre of the Earth was really like? William found it all very annoying. And William's teacher found his questions very annoying, too.

Then, one day, Mrs Martin had a brainwave. She told William all about *evidence*.

"You see, William," she said, "if we aren't sure that something is true, we can use evidence to check it. Evidence can be drawings or photographs. It can be birth certificates or videos."

After that, William began to enjoy the idea of using real things to show what was true. He was very upset when Grandma refused to show him her birth certificate.

"It's for evidence," cried William. "I need it to back up my family history project."

But she said no. Grandad was much more helpful. He let William borrow his birth certificate and take it to school.

"Of course, he's much older than me," said Grandma.

But the subject that William found most difficult of all was English. Again and again, Mrs Martin asked him to make up a story about something. But William didn't understand why he should write something that wasn't true.

"What's the point?" he asked.

"It helps your imagination to grow," sighed Mrs Martin. "I'm sure you make up lots of wonderful stories in your head, William. We just want to hear some of them."

"I don't make up any stories in my head," replied William. "Why would I want to do that? It wouldn't be true. You can't trust made-up things."

"Well, in a way you're right," replied his teacher. "You don't have to believe them. But you can enjoy them. And sometimes they're true in other ways. If you read a story about a boy being afraid of a ghost, it doesn't mean that there really are ghosts. It doesn't mean that there really was a boy who was afraid of them. But it does mean that people are often afraid of things they don't really understand. That's true, even if the story isn't. Do you see?"

But William didn't see at all. "I'll write a diary instead," he said. "It will be a sort of story, but it will be true."

Mrs Martin sighed and agreed. She thought a diary was better than nothing.

One day, Mrs Martin said that she had something exciting to tell the class.

"Starting today, you are going to stop writing lots of different stories," she said. "Instead, each of you is going to write one long story, like a proper book. You will write a chapter each week. At the end of term, a famous author is going to come and read the books. She will give prizes for the most imaginative stories."

All the children were very excited – all except one, of course. William was frowning.

"I don't know why I have to bother," he said. "Mine isn't going to be imaginative at all. I'm going to keep writing my diary."

"Well, if that is what you feel happy doing, that will be fine," said Mrs Martin. But it didn't make *her* feel happy. She had read dozens and dozens of William's 'stories'. All of them were written like a diary. And all of them were very, very boring.

"Today I got up at half-past seven. I had a cup of tea. Then I had cereal and an orange for breakfast. It was raining when I set off for school, so I wore my raincoat. I looked at my rain counter and saw that two centimetres of rain had fallen overnight. I told Mrs Martin at school, but she didn't seem very interested. James Jones stole my pencil. We had cheese salad and apple pie for lunch. I got A+ for my maths homework. It was still raining when I went home."

Mrs Martin thought of having to read a whole book full of this kind of thing and sighed. She did not like the thought at all. But it looked as if that was what she would have to do. William would only write about things he knew were true, and that was the end of it.

But William's life was about to change in the most amazing way.

That evening, after he had eaten his dinner (and recorded every mouthful in his new 'story' diary), William sat down at the desk in his room to do his homework. It was maths, which he liked. He was doing a difficult sum about how long it would take three men to dig five holes. It was a very interesting problem. So at first he didn't notice the little puffs of smoke coming from his pencil-case.

When he saw the smoke, William looked down at his pencil-case in horror. He had learnt about fire safety in school. His pencils must be on fire! He knew he shouldn't open the zip, in case the fire spread. William ran into the bathroom, filled a glass with water, ran back into his room and threw it over the pencil-case. (He remembered to move his maths homework out of the way first.) The smoke stopped at once, but then something even odder happened. The pencil-case started to cough.

William watched it in amazement.

The pencil-case gave a little jump with each cough. William thought as fast as he could. But he could only think of one reason for his pencil-case to be jumping up and down. There must be something (very small) inside it.

William felt sure that there must be a mouse inside his pencil-case. He had never seen a mouse at school, but he knew that they liked living under the floorboards in old buildings. William's school was a very old building. And it had lots of floorboards. A mouse could have crept in at school and been chewing his pencils ever since. Maybe it wasn't smoke he had seen. Maybe it was puffs of sawdust or something like that.

William didn't like the idea of a mouse running about in his bedroom. So he picked up the dripping pencil-case and carefully carried it into the bathroom. He shut the door firmly (and locked it), and put the jumping pencil-case down in the basin. Then, very, very slowly, he pulled back the zip.

What he saw next was about the same size as a mouse, but it wasn't a mouse. William knew that mice are not green and orange with wings. He thought it must be a bat. It had to be some kind of fruit-eating bat from a tropical country. William decided to go back to his room to look up the creature in his nature encyclopedia. But, just at that moment, the animal gave a final cough, and little puffs of white smoke started to come out of its nose.

William's mind was racing. He could remember a lesson from school about animals called salamanders, and a story that they live in fires. But salamanders didn't have wings, like this creature. And anyway, that was just a story. It wasn't true. It was because salamanders often live in dead logs. When the logs are thrown onto a fire, the salamanders run out. This little animal wasn't running anywhere. It looked perfectly happy.

William hurried out of the bathroom and shut the door carefully behind him. He rushed to his room and found his magnifying glass. When he was back in the bathroom, he looked at the creature again. This time, he was going to be scientific. There must be a way to find out what it was.

It was a long time before William could believe what his eyes were telling him. When he used the magnifying glass, he could see that it wasn't only smoke that was coming from the creature's nostrils. There were tiny flames as well. He could see that its green and orange skin was made up of tiny scales. He could see that it had a long tail with a forked bit on the end. He could see that the tiny animal sitting quietly in the basin was not a mouse. It was not a fruit-bat. It was not a salamander. ***It was a dragon.***

You know, and I know, and William knew that dragons are not ***real***, in the way that cows and pigs are real. Dragons are imaginary, like fairies and goblins and unicorns. You can only find them in storybooks. But William also knew that one of these storybook creatures was sitting in his bathroom basin. He needed to do some serious thinking – and fast!

You or I might have been puzzled about the whole thing. So puzzled that our brains refused to take in what we were seeing. So puzzled that we couldn't think slowly and sensibly about it afterwards. But, as you know, William was a pretty clever boy. After a couple of minutes of hard thinking, he found that it was all very simple.

How did he know that there were no such things as dragons? He knew because books and teachers had told him so. Did he believe everything that he read in books or was told by teachers? No! Did he believe things he could see to be true with his own eyes? Definitely! There was no question about it. There was a tiny dragon in his bathroom. That was real evidence. It proved that there are such things as dragons in real life. The only problem now was deciding what to do next.

"I wish that I knew what dragons like to eat," said William. He always talked out loud when he had a problem to solve. "At least, I think that big dragons like to eat people, but what could this one manage?" He peered again at the creature.

"Mmmmnnnng," said the dragon, with its mouth full. It was very hungry. So it had answered the question itself by tucking in to the soap. William was not sure that soap was a very good meal for anyone, dragon or human. But the dragon seemed perfectly happy. Half a bar of soap disappeared into its tiny mouth. Then it sat down and made what sounded very like a burp. William thought that the creature must now be thirsty. He knew that he would be very thirsty if he had just eaten half a bar of soap. So he turned on the cold tap and just a little trickle of water came out of it.

But at once, a tiny screeching came from the basin. The dragon started to jump about, trying to keep away from the water. William bent down. It wasn't screeching. The dragon was talking, but in a very, very tiny voice.

"Turn it off! Turn it off!" the dragon was squeaking. "Don't you know anything? Turn it off!"

William did as he was told. Then he leaned down again and asked, "Why?"

"Dragons hate water!" squealed the dragon. "It puts out our flames! And they're so difficult to light again. And that reminds me..."

"Oh," William knew what the dragon was going to say. "I'm sorry about throwing the water over you earlier. I thought my pencil-case was on fire."

"That was pretty silly," said the dragon. "What on earth made you think that?"

"The smoke," said William crossly. He didn't like being told he was silly by a creature that was not much bigger than his nose. "*Your* smoke," he added.

"Ah, well, I suppose I can see your point," said the dragon. "That could have been the reason for the smoke. But didn't you even *think* that it might have been a dragon?"

"Of course not," replied William. "I didn't know there were such things as dragons."

"Didn't know?" cried the dragon. "But I know for a fact that there are dozens of children's stories with dragons in them. How could you possibly not know? Can't you read?"

"Of course I can!" William was getting even crosser now. "But those stories are made up. The things in them aren't true, you know."

"Really?" the dragon laughed. "So how do you explain me, then?"

William couldn't.

The dragon stayed with William for almost two months. He never showed himself when anyone else was around. But when William was alone, the dragon came out. They had long conversations. The dragon told William all about what it was like to be a dragon. He described how it felt to fly so high up in the sky that Earth looked like a blue and green dot. William heard how the dragons meet once a year on the high, cold mountains, and start fires to keep themselves warm. He found out what dragons dream about. He listened to the strange, roaring, hissing songs that dragons sing when they are together.

His new friend told him how much fun

it was to be a dragon. He explained how dragons stay hidden from human beings. He told him all about chasing eagles through the blue sky and burning their tail feathers off. "Eagles always think they know it all," laughed the dragon. "Sometimes you have to teach them a lesson."

He told William the stories that dragons tell each other on cold winter nights – funny stories about stupid human beings who get eaten up, scary stories about fierce dragon-slayers, exciting stories about treasure caves full of gold and silver. And William wrote down every word of these conversations in his diary.

Those two months changed William's life. He had to think again about lots of things, such as whether you could believe what you read in books, and what it really meant to say that something was true. He started to notice things he had never noticed before. He saw the way that clouds sometimes looked like dragons. He noticed that there seemed to be a man smiling in the moon. He knew that the clouds *weren't* dragons and that there wasn't *really* a man in the moon. But he started to understand that it could be fun to think about things that only *seemed* to be true. His family, his teachers and his friends thought that he was much, much easier to be around. He liked them better, too.

At the end of term, the famous author came into school to choose the best stories. She chose William's diary as "The story showing the most imagination". He was amazed. He couldn't tell Mrs Martin that every word of it was true! He was even more amazed when he saw how happy everyone else was for him. It felt really good. He liked it so much, he didn't notice that the dragon had gone – completely.

William searched for the dragon for a long time. He even searched in those places you'd rather not look, like the darker corners of the bathroom and inside his brother's trainers. But there was no sign of the dragon.

Sometimes, William felt sure that out of the

corner of his eye he could see little flickering flames and puffs of smoke. But, however fast he turned around, they were never really there.

The dragon had disappeared forever. But William knew he would never forget the wonderful things it had taught him. And on cold, frosty mornings, when his breath looks like little puffs of smoke, he wears a secret smile.

The Alien Headteacher

All headteachers are a bit odd in some way. It goes with the job. But Mr Bleaks was much, much odder than any other headteacher the children had known. He was even odder than their old head, Mrs Glood. She used to wear strange stripy tights and her hair was a different colour every week. She rode a bike that looked like it was made hundreds of years ago. But she wasn't as deeply, strangely and weirdly odd as Mr Bleaks.

The headteacher sometimes muttered to himself in a foreign language. There were children at the school who spoke lots of different languages, but none of them recognized the words that Mr Bleaks said.

He had really *liked* the semolina served up in the school cafeteria. He had even had second helpings. But everyone knew that school dinners were disgusting. At a school football match, the children had heard him shout, "Come on, the Blues!" even though one team was wearing yellow and the home team was in red. Who was he talking to? What did it all mean?

Everyone liked Mr Bleaks, and that was strange too. The children had never *liked* a headteacher before. But Mr Bleaks was different. He remembered everyone's name. He never lost his temper. He even tried to make lessons fun!

For weeks, Rosie and her friends had tried to work out why their headteacher was so very strange, but they had failed. They had thought as hard as they could, but it was no use. Nothing could explain why Mr Bleaks was so odd. Then, that morning, Patrick had an amazing idea.

"Maybe," he said, "he's an alien!"

Patrick had been reading a space story and at first the others just laughed at him. But Patrick made them listen. It explained a lot when they thought about it.

"You see," said Patrick, "if he was from another planet, he'd probably have been programmed to act like a headteacher. Or at least, what the aliens think a headteacher is like. So that's why he keeps getting it a bit wrong. He probably learned about shouting 'Come on, the Blues!' but they didn't know that you have to change it to match the colour of the team you're supporting."

"It would explain the semolina, too," said Megan. "I expect all Earth food tastes the same to aliens. He wouldn't know he wasn't supposed to like it."

"It would make sense of the funny

language," said Noah. He looked very excited. "Sometimes he must forget and start talking Alien!"

Rosie frowned and looked around at her friends. They were all sitting on the grass in front of the school. Everyone looked interested.

"I bet we're right," said Patrick. "Mr Bleaks is an alien."

"Yes, but I don't see how we can know. Not for sure," Rosie said.

The others sighed.

"What we need," she went on, "is an alien test. We have to think of something that will show if he's human. Something that will prove it."

"In films, they test to see whether the alien has real human feelings," said Patrick. "Like, they find out if he would cry if his dog died, that sort of thing."

The others looked at Patrick and laughed.

"We can't go around killing off old Bleaks's dog," said Rosie. "What else do they try in films?"

"Well, sometimes they peel the skin off to see if there is machinery underneath. If there is, he's definitely an alien."

"I can't see that working, Patrick," said Rosie with a smile. "'Excuse me, Mr Bleaks, do you mind if I just peel your skin back to see if you're really an alien? It won't take a moment.'"

Everyone giggled, except for Noah. He was looking very serious.

"You're right," he said. "I think it's

really important that he doesn't find out that we know. He's been very nice so far, but that's because he thinks we believe him. Who knows what he might do if we find out the truth?"

"That's a good point, *if* he's an alien. But we don't actually ***know***, do we?" said Rosie. "I still think we need to come up with some tests. An alien planet can't have taught him everything he needs to know about Earth. If we could ask him some really detailed questions about *little* things, we might find out if he grew up here. If he is an alien, he's sure to get lots of answers wrong."

"I think that's a good idea," said Megan. "We should all think of lots of questions to ask him. Things that he wouldn't know unless he grew up here."

"In the meantime," said Noah, "we should just start making a list of all the odd things we notice. You never know, there might be a kind of pattern."

Over the next few days, the friends began to make their plans. Megan asked her mother about which children's television programmes were popular when she was young. She thought her mum might be about the same age as Mr Bleaks. If he were really an alien, he wouldn't know anything about old television programmes.

"Why on earth do you want to know what I used to watch on TV?" asked her mother.

"It's for a history project," Megan explained.

"Megan," said her mother, "I don't want to feel as if I'm already part of history. I'm not even 40 yet. Go and ask your dad. I expect he'll be more helpful. I bet he watched a lot more TV than I did."

Megan's dad didn't mind being asked.

He told Megan about lots and lots of old TV programmes. Megan had to stop him talking so she could go to bed.

After that, every time she met Mr Bleaks, Megan asked one of her questions about old television programmes.

"My dad was telling me about *The Adventure of the Blue Hand*," she said, "but he couldn't remember the name of the little boy with the parrot. I expect you remember, Mr Bleaks."

"No, I don't," said the headteacher.

The next day, Megan tried again. "How many dogs were there in *Bonzo's Band*?" she asked. "I bet you loved that cartoon, Mr Bleaks. My dad says it was his favourite."

"No, I never saw it," said Mr Bleaks. Megan thought he looked a bit embarrassed.

Megan decided to write down everything she asked Mr Bleaks in a notebook. She was careful to write down how he looked as well as what he said. But she didn't get any answers to her questions.

"Did you ever watch a programme called ***The Family Ghost***?" Megan asked her headteacher on Wednesday. "Dad can't remember if the ghost was called Gordon or Gregory. Do you remember, Mr Bleaks?"

"I have no idea," said Mr Bleaks. And he rushed away before Megan could ask him another question.

Finally, on Friday, Megan asked Mr Bleaks about the words that Elmo the Pirate Cat always shouted as he went into battle. Mr Bleaks gave a loud sigh and looked down at her.

"Megan," he said, "every day this week you have asked me something about old TV programmes from years and years ago. Why do you keep asking me all these things? I don't know the answers to any of your questions. When I grew up, we didn't have a TV. Why don't you ask one of the other teachers instead?"

Megan wrote down everything he had said in her notebook. She couldn't wait to tell the others all about it.

After school that day, the friends met on the grass in front of the school gates. They were all ready to swap information. Megan told them about the questions she had been asking Mr Bleaks all week. When she told them what he had said that afternoon, everyone gasped.

"Of course, that's what he *would* say,"

said Rosie, "if he was an alien. He couldn't know the answers to all those questions, but it took him until Friday to think of an excuse. And it's not even a very good excuse. I mean, ***everyone*** has a TV, don't they?"

"But it's ages ago that Mr Bleaks was young," said Noah. "Maybe there weren't many televisions around then. He ***might*** have said that because he's an alien. But he might have said it because it is true. I don't think this proves anything. What have you found out, Rosie?"

Rosie looked very pleased with herself. She pulled a piece of paper out of her bag.

"I've made a list," she said, "of all the odd things he's done this week. Listen.

1. He ate those horrible hard peas at lunch on Monday. Nobody ever eats them.

2. He wore odd socks, one green and one red, on Tuesday.

3. He didn't shout when James stuck chewing gum to his shoes on Wednesday.

4. (This is a good one.) He took Luke's model spaceship on Thursday and *kept it in his office*.

5. He didn't know the words to 'The Wheels on the Bus' on Friday."

"Really? Everyone knows the words to 'The Wheels on the Bus'!" cried Noah.

"Not," said Rosie, "if you didn't grow up on planet Earth."

There was silence while the friends thought about the news.

"The evidence is building up," said

Patrick. He had moved on from space stories to detective stories. "None of these things would mean anything by itself. But when you add them all together, it looks like Mr Bleaks really is an alien!"

Megan frowned. "It does look bad for him," she said, "but he's such a nice man. When I was annoying him with all my questions, he didn't tell me to go away or be quiet. Mrs Glood would have done that. And she wouldn't have been nice about it."

The others nodded. Mr Bleaks was a much better headteacher than Mrs Glood.

"Well, we're not saying there's anything wrong with being an alien," said Noah. He always tried to be fair. "It's just that it would be good to know for certain. I'm not sure why, exactly."

"I am!" cried Patrick. "It would be exciting! We would be in the newspapers and on television and everything. We'd be famous! Everyone would want to know what it is like being taught by a real, live alien. We'd probably get rich! Newspapers would pay us for our stories."

They all thought about what it would be like to be famous.

"People would visit us from all over the world!" said Megan.

"He might even take us to visit his planet!" added Noah.

"All right," said Rosie. "We must try even harder to find out for certain. Has anyone got any ideas?"

There was a long silence. Then Noah said, "What about his DNA? We could get it tested."

Noah's father was a doctor, so he knew more about science and tests than the others.

"What's DNA?" asked Megan.

"I'm not sure," said Noah. "All I know

is that everyone has it and everyone's is different. You can have your DNA tested to find out if you're related to someone else. Dad gets it done for people sometimes."

Megan didn't understand at all.

"I like Mr Bleaks, but I don't want to be related to him," she said. "Not if he hasn't got a TV. What would there be to do if you went to stay?"

"No one's saying you have to be related to him," said Noah. "In fact, if he's an alien, you definitely ***can't*** be related to him. That's what I thought. Aliens ***must*** have different DNA from human beings, mustn't they? If we could get it tested, then we'd know for sure."

The children looked at each other. Knowing for sure seemed like a very good idea.

"How would you get him to sit the exam?" asked Megan.

"It's not that sort of test," said Noah. "You have to test his blood. We just need a tiny bit of blood."

The others looked at him and shook their heads.

"Are you out of your mind?" asked Rosie. "How can we get a teacher's blood? 'Hello, Mr Bleaks, I've got a knife here. Put your hand out, please.'"

"It is never, ever going to work," said Patrick. "And I don't want to go around sticking knives in people. You can forget it, Noah."

"He might fall over or something and bleed a bit," said Noah. "Then we could get some of his blood and he wouldn't notice."

"Have you ever seen a teacher fall over?" asked Rosie. "They don't move fast enough to fall over."

Noah sighed. It had seemed like such a good idea, but they were right. There was no way of getting Mr Bleaks's blood. They would have to think of something else.

"Let's think about it over the weekend," said Rosie. "We can't give up. There *must* be a way of testing him."

The friends went home, but they didn't feel very happy. It seemed as if they were really stuck.

But on Monday morning, Noah ran into school with shining eyes and a great big smile.

"We've got to meet behind the art block at lunchtime," he whispered to Rosie and Patrick. "Tell Megan! I've got news."

Mr Bleaks was standing nearby, so they couldn't ask Noah any questions. The morning seemed to crawl by. But at last the lunchtime bell rang. The friends rushed out to meet Noah, and his news was worth waiting for.

"The thing is," said Noah, "I talked to Dad about testing DNA. And he told me that we don't need blood! Any part of the person's body will do."

"What do you suggest? An ear? Half a finger?" asked Rosie.

"No! It could be a fingernail or a bit of hair," said Noah. "It could even be some spit, but I don't see how we can get that."

"I don't see how we can get the other bits either," said Megan.

"I think the hair is the easiest." Noah had been thinking about this all weekend, and he had a plan. "There are sure to be some hairs on the collar of his coat. We just have to sneak into his office and get some."

The friends thought about the idea.

"I think it could work," said Rosie. "I could do it after school, when he's in the playground making sure everyone goes home. Give me a couple of days. I'll sneak in and get the hairs."

But the next morning, two things happened that changed everything.

First of all, Noah came in looking very upset. He told them that DNA tests cost hundreds of pounds. There was no way they could afford to do the test. It seemed as if they were never going to find out the truth.

"So we're back at the beginning," Patrick sighed. "We have to think of a test that doesn't cost money."

The second thing that happened was a big surprise. Mr Bleaks called the whole school together in the gym for a special assembly.

"I've called you in here to talk about something very important," said the

headteacher. "I expect you've seen the reports on the news about the terrible fighting that is taking place over in Estavia. Lots of people have lost their homes. They are living in tents. There is fighting everywhere. They can't escape and they can't go back to their homes. They have no food and no money. It is up to people like us, who have so much, to help them. I'm starting a collection for them today. They need food, clothing and medical supplies. Noah, I'm coming to see your father tonight. He has promised to help. I'd like all the rest of you to go home and see what you can give to help children just like you. Books, toys, old clothes – anything will be useful."

The headteacher paused and took a deep breath.

"Some of you may wonder why I am doing this," he said. "Well, I grew up in Estavia. When I was a boy there, we were very poor. Then a war started and we lost even the few things we had. I know what it is like to be caught in the middle of fighting. We were always scared and hungry. We ate anything we could find, even weeds from the side of the road. My parents were killed in the war, but I was lucky. I was helped by people just like you in a country far away. They sent me toys, clothes and books. They took care of me, even though they didn't know me. Later I was able to leave Estavia. I came to school here. I learned to speak English (although I still forget sometimes) and I have had a very happy life. But I can't stand by and see the same thing happening all over again. I have to try to help the children out in Estavia. Just like those people helped me when I was a child."

There was silence for a moment. Mr Bleaks looked a bit nervous. Then the hall was filled with children shouting, "We'll help! Don't worry!" They picked up the leaflets that the headteacher had made for them to take home. Everyone wanted to help.

When they met up outside the gates that afternoon, the four friends felt a bit silly.

"It explains the funny language," said Megan.

"It explains eating semolina and horrible hard peas," said Noah. "Even those must taste better than weeds."

"And it explains not having a TV," added Rosie.

"But there is something it doesn't explain," said Patrick. "What about 'Come on, the Blues!' and the odd socks?"

"Did you say odd socks?" asked a friendly voice. "Have I done it again?"

The headteacher had walked up behind them as they were talking. He looked down at his feet and sighed.

"I'm colour blind, you see," he said. "I've never been any different, so I don't mind. But I do make mistakes sometimes. Why are you all laughing?"

Russell's Grandad

Russell was spending the weekend with his dad. As usual, they were going to the football match on Saturday afternoon followed by a takeaway. On Sunday, if the weather was dry, they would play football in the park. If it was wet they would go swimming.

Russell was glad that he could see his dad at the weekends. His dad would pick him up on Friday after school and take him back to his mum on Sunday evening. It worked out very well for Russell because, although he was sad not to see his parents together any more, he did enjoy having two homes, even though they were very different.

But as time went on, Russell began to notice that he never got to see his grandad any more. Russell was very fond of his grandad. For a start, he could run almost as fast as Russell. And not many grandads could do that. He also claimed that he could do cartwheels. And, although Russell had never actually seen him do one, he believed him.

Russell liked spending time with his grandad. He took Russell fishing. He told him stories about how things were a long time ago, and he showed him how to do magic tricks. So Russell felt really sad not to see his grandad any more.

On Sunday morning, when Russell was eating his breakfast cereal, he suddenly thought of his grandad and said, "How come I never see Grandad anymore?"

Dad, who was reading the back of the cereal packet, looked up in surprise.

"Er...mm...er...oh, haven't you?" he finally managed to stammer out.

"No, I haven't," Russell replied. "Am I going to?"

"Of course you will, Russell," said Dad. "You just have to give it a little more time. Your mother and I are still sorting things out."

A few weeks later he asked his mother the same question. "How come I never see Grandad any more?"

The question surprised her.

"Oh, don't you?" And then she answered her own question. "Come to think of it, I guess you don't." She started to apologize. "It's just that we're all so busy that we never really find time to arrange things like that."

"Will I ever see him again?"

"Of course you will, Russell," she answered, looking slightly hurt. "Of course you will." But she didn't say when. And Russell noticed that she didn't mention the subject again.

And after a while, neither did Russell.

One night Russell was woken up by a tapping sound at his window. He ran over and pulled open the curtain. He couldn't believe what he saw. "GRANDAD!" he shouted, forgetting that it was the middle of the night. "What are you doing here?"

"I thought it'd be nice to see you," Grandad replied, giving his grandson a big smile. He could tell that Russell was genuinely pleased to see him and that made him happy. "Here, I brought you a few things." He reached into his coat pocket and brought out a false moustache, three tin soldiers and an old fountain pen. "Be careful with the pen," he said. "It leaks."

"But how did you get up here?"

"I climbed up a drainpipe."

"Isn't that dangerous?"

"Nothing like what we did during the war."

"It's great to see you, Grandad. I missed you." And he went over and gave his grandad a hug.

"I missed you too," Grandad replied. "It's not much fun fishing alone."

"Let's have a midnight feast," Russell suggested. And he reached for his special tin.

They ate sweets and talked about fishing and football and how large dinosaurs grew. But it was getting late, and

Grandad could see that Russell was getting tired. As much as he hated to leave, he knew the time had come. He got up slowly and said, "Well, Russell, I'm afraid it's time to go." He began tying his scarf around his neck.

"Oh, Grandad, do you really have to?"

"I'm afraid so. All good things have to come to an end." And as he talked he walked towards the window and pulled it open.

Russell thought there was something very funny about watching his grandad leave by the window. "Will I see you again?" he asked.

"Oh, yes, you'll see me all right, but you might have to look twice," his grandad answered. And he gave him his special wink just before shutting the window.

The following week Russell's mother took him to the circus. That was one of her special treats for him because she knew how much he loved it. And it only came to town once a year. What Russell loved best of all was the animals. The elephants always seemed so much larger at the circus than they did at the zoo. And it always amazed him how one man with just a crack of a whip could keep a cage full of lions under control.

He sat through it all, the clowns, the jugglers, the death-defying trapeze artists that his mother couldn't bear to look at (she always turned away when they jumped off their swings and connected with their partners in mid-air) and, of course, the animals. He cheered as loudly as anyone when they all took their bows at the end of the performance. But on this day the ringmaster announced at the end of the show that everyone was welcome to meet the clowns backstage.

"Oh, can we, Mum? That would be brilliant!" Russell asked.

"You go," his mother said, "while I talk to Mrs Williams. I'll see you outside, but try not to be too long."

Russell raced to the back of the tent. A crowd of autograph hunters had gathered there. Roars of laughter rang out as the clowns played tricks on the children, making pens disappear and reappear in the strangest places, and tossing them into the air only to catch them on their noses.

Russell was waiting on tiptoe, trying to see over the heads of the crowd, when he heard his name.

"Russell!"

He turned, wondering how many other Russells there were in the tent. "I must be the only one," he thought, because nobody else had turned around. He looked around but found it hard to tell where the voice was coming from. It wasn't very loud and for a second he wondered whether he had imagined it. He looked behind him.

"No, over here."

Perhaps it was another trick, he thought.

"Not there, here!" the voice said. And this time he knew he wasn't making it up.

He looked over his shoulder at the trapeze artists. But no sooner had he taken two steps towards them than he heard the voice again.

"No, over here," it commanded.

Now he was becoming really confused. Where could it possibly be coming from? It couldn't be coming from the big drum. Or could it? Once again he changed direction.

"You're getting closer," the voice said encouragingly.

Russell took another step towards a corner that was full of musical instruments and circus equipment. Then he noticed a curious thing. Right at the back stood a pantomime horse all on his own. And it suddenly dawned on him not only where the voice was coming from, but whose voice it was.

"GRANDAD!" he blurted out as he came closer.

"So you finally caught on," his grandad said.

"What are you doing here?" Russell couldn't believe what he was seeing, or that he was actually talking to a horse (or what looked like a horse, anyway).

"You were always one for the circus and I heard you might be dropping by," his grandad said. "I thought it would be nice to see you, even though I can't see you very well."

"But how did you...I mean...what?" Russell was becoming flustered. And people were also starting to give him some funny looks.

His grandad realized that this was not the best place to hold a conversation.

"I'll tell you some other time," he said. "I'm not going to talk too long because people will think you're daft talking to a horse. Besides, you don't want to keep your mother waiting. You know what she's like when she gets annoyed. So you had better move along. In the meantime, keep your eyes open."

"Why do you say that?" Russell wasn't quite sure what he meant.

"You never know what you'll see next. Bye, Russell."

"Bye, Grandad. See you soon, I hope."

"What took you so long?" his mother said when he got back. "You've been gone for some time. Did you run into one of your friends?"

"I met a lovely old horse," Russell said, laughing as he said it, "and I chatted to him for a while."

"Really, Russell, talking to horses! What will you think of next?"

A few weeks later Russell and his friend Jack were coming home from school when they noticed a new ice-cream man on the street.

"He looks a bit old to be an ice-cream man," Jack said.

"You're never too old to be an ice-cream man," Russell replied.

They strolled over and ordered two cornets. The man served them and they both reached into their pockets to pay when, to their great surprise, they heard the ice-cream man say, "That's all right boys, this one's on me."

Russell was surprised by the man's generosity, especially since he didn't even know them. He looked up to thank him and it suddenly dawned on him who it was.

"GRANDAD!"

"Hello, Russell, I said you'd see me again, didn't I?" And I was right.

"I know, but I didn't recognize you at first."

"I'm not surprised. People often don't when you're wearing a uniform. It throws them off." And he smiled as he got back into the van and drove off.

In the following months Russell saw quite a bit of his grandad.

Once he was a clown at the fairground.

Another time he was Father Christmas, which surprised everyone because it was the middle of May.

But these meetings didn't always work out smoothly. And things sometimes took an unexpected turn. Like the time when Russell saw a new park keeper at his local park. He rushed right over and tried to pull off the man's moustache, yelling, "I know who you are, I know who you are. You're not fooling me!"

But the moustache didn't come off. And, when the man began screaming with pain, a very embarrassed Russell could only mumble, "I'm sorry, I thought you were somebody else."

"Well, be a little more careful next time," the man said, looking hurt as well as angry.

But usually he was quite good at seeing through the disguises. So, when Russell's mum took him to meet his dad at the Hotel Splendide for a birthday treat, he spotted the new doorman straight away. He walked right over to him and said, "Hello, Grandad!"

And sure enough that's who it was. "Hello, Russell," his grandad replied. "You're becoming quite good at this."

"Well, you're giving me a lot of practice," Russell answered.

"And, as we all know, practice makes perfect."

Russell's mum hurried over.

"Come along, Russell dear," she said, smiling politely at the doorman. "You really shouldn't be talking to strangers," she added in a whisper. "I don't know how many times I've told you."

When Russell's dad saw them talking to the doorman, he quickly joined them.

"Is there a problem?" he asked, looking worried.

Russell couldn't help laughing. And once he started he couldn't stop. His grandad was smiling too, but he was better at hiding it.

"Could somebody please tell me what is so funny?" asked Russell's dad, looking rather cross.

"You mean you don't know?" Russell giggled.

"Of course I don't know. Just what is it that I'm supposed to know?" He was becoming even more cross now, thinking his son was playing him for a fool.

"Don't you recognize him?" Russell asked.

"Recognize who?"

Russell pointed to the doorman.

"I'm sorry, I'm not an expert on doormen. One looks pretty much like another to me. Is there something special about this particular one?"

"It's Grandad!" Russell said, still laughing.

His mother looked startled. She stared hard at the doorman's face, but she still couldn't work it out. She leaned over to get a closer look so she could inspect him more closely. She looked directly at him for what seemed like a long time. "Why, so it is," she finally said, sounding very surprised. "Grandad, what are you doing here?"

Grandad smiled and said, "That's how we meet, Russell and I."

Russell's mother looked upset. "But you know you can come to the house whenever you like. We're always happy to see you."

Grandad adjusted his hat and looked down to the ground. "Well, you know how it is," he said. "I didn't want to impose. And with his dad not being there I felt, well, a bit funny."

Just then, Russell's special birthday tea arrived. While they ate, Russell told his mother about all the different disguises that Grandad had used. She listened carefully and, even though she didn't want to, she had to laugh.

"Now you listen here, Grandad," she said. "I don't want you meeting like this any more. You know we'd love to see you, you're part of the family."

"It's just that we've been very busy..." started Russell's dad.

"Oh, never mind that. From now on," Russell's mum said firmly, "you must visit us whenever you want to."

"And no more of these silly disguises," said Russell's dad. "Will you promise me that?"

"I promise," Grandad said, "that after today there will be no more disguises."

"Thank you," said Dad. "I'm very relieved to hear it."

"Good!" said Mum. "That settles that.

Now, Russell, it's getting late. I think we had better take the bus home."

They made their way to the bus stop and waited, and waited, along with everybody else.

By the time the bus arrived it was almost dark. And, when they finally got on and heard the driver say, "Fares please," Russell couldn't help noticing that above his big smile was a moustache that was slightly askew.